To those who long to fly and those who are learning to listen.

"For whether it be a strong wire rope or a slender and delicate thread that holds the bird, it matters not; for until the cord be broken the bird cannot fly."

-St. John of The Cross

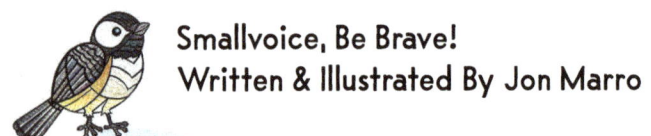

Smallvoice, Be Brave!
Written & Illustrated By Jon Marro

Copyright © 2020 Jon Marro
Independently Published By:

WORLDS WITHIN
BOOKS

Worlds Within Enterprises, LLC
www.worldswithin.com

All rights reserved. No part of this publication may be reproduced, distributed, or transmitted in any form or by any means, including photocopying, recording, or other electronic or mechanical methods, without the prior written permission of the publisher, except in the case of brief quotations embodied in critical reviews and certain other noncommercial uses permitted by copyright law. For permission requests, write to the publisher, addressed "Attention: Permissions Coordinator," at the website address above.

Ordering Information: For information about special discounts for bulk purchases and wholesale, please contact the publisher at the website address listed above.

Courageously edited by my wingwomen: Blair Wojcik & Eva Ackerman.

In Loving memory of my Dad, Bob Marro. As your spirit left your body it inspired this book. Love you.
Special Thanks to Ted Bizzarro for your brotherhood, loyalty and KindhearTEDness. You helped this hatch.
To Mom and Kevin for being my birdhouse and feeding me and the Chickadees so well.
And to Vermont, for always being home, no matter how far I wandered.

Printed by Ingram Spark (www.ingramspark.com) in the United States of America.

First Printing: 2020

ISBN 978-1-7341906-0-1 (Hardcover)
ISBN 978-1-7341906-2-5 (Paperback)
ISBN 978-1-7341906-5-6 (eBook)

Written & Illustrated by
JON MARRO

There once was a Chickadee named Smallvoice,
Who was determined to face his fear.
He heard a small voice inside of him
That nobody else could hear.

"Do not be afraid," the voice would say,
"Even if things seem grave
Your courage is always inside of you
Be Brave, Smallvoice. Be Brave!"

Smallvoice lived with his cautious folks
On a hillside country farm.
Through it ran a long, dirt road,
Dividing their nest from a barn.

Their neighbor was a Woodpecker
Whose hair was spiked bright-red.
He fixed things up around their home,
And his name was Kindheart Ted.

Behind the barn there was a meadow
With food for all four seasons -
Where Smallvoice was told to never go.
His parents had their reasons.

Atop the barn was perched an owl
Who never said a word.
He sat and watched the road for mice
Or some daring, foolish bird.

"Smallvoice!" his mother chirped,
"You cannot cross that road!
Remember your father's famous tale,
Ten thousand times he's told?"

Smallvoice tucked his tail and rolled his eyes
As his father did recite
The story which he knew began:
"It was a dark and stormy night..."

"...The beast flew off,
Some thought for good,
But returned and took his seat.
So, if we try to cross that road
It is us he'll surely eat!

That is why we live right here,
On this side of the path.
We are safe inside our birdhouse
With our feeder and bird bath."

Days passed, seasons changed,
And though Smallvoice had no choice,
"There is life beyond the world you know,"
Came whispering that voice.

His intuition spoke to him:
"Something's not quite right.
For never in my few short years,
Has that owl taken flight."

Then one frosty winter's day
From out beneath a Cedar,
Raced a hungry, clumsy
Big-tailed squirrel
Who toppled their birdfeeder.

Seeds and nuts were scattered
All across the snowy lawn.
The Chickadee's food for the long, cold winter
Was suddenly, now, all gone.

As Smallvoice watched the seeds get eaten
By birds who'd taken charge,
The small voice that lived inside of him,
Suddenly grew quite LARGE.

He puffed his chest, he stomped his feet
And raised his beak real proud,
"THAT IS IT! - I'm not afraid!"
Smallvoice said out loud.

With desperate times upon him,
He called the Owl's bluff
As the feeding frenzy snowballed,
Smallvoice had had enough!

Past the frozen fence he marched,
He now had things to prove.
But Hungry Eyes seemed not to care,
Not a feather on him moved.

Smallvoice reached the big red barn,
Topped with ice and snow.
His small voice calmly whispered:
"You are braver than you know."

He made his way atop the roof
Climbing a Cypress then a Fir
His tiny legs were shaking
Still, the owl did not stir

When Smallvoice reached the snowy peak,
What he saw was quite fantastic.
There was nothing to fear - as his small voice said,
The owl was made of plastic!

This Hungry Eyes was just a fake,
Made to scare away most pests.
Smallvoice's inner wisdom
Had worked out for the best.

Winterberries grew fat and red
Dangling from the tree,
And in the meadow was a harvest,
As far as his eyes could see.

As Smallvoice gathered feasts of food
He danced in festive fun,
Then he whistled down triumphantly,
"There's plenty, everyone!"

Above the barn was a perfect place
For the Chickadee's new nest,
So his parents invited all the neighbors
As their special dinner guests.

Flowers bloomed and food was shared,
New tales were being told -
About the tiny bird with the biggest heart
Who dared to cross the road.

And to this humble hero
Their gratitude they gave,
As they sang in celebration:
"Be Brave, Smallvoice!
Be Brave!"

CPSIA information can be obtained
at www.ICGtesting.com
Printed in the USA
LVHW072242020221
678126LV00005B/123